Raven Brings Back the Sun

A TALE FROM CANADA

Retold by Suzanne I. Barchers
Illustrated by Angela Oliynyk

RED
CHAIR
•PRESS•

Please visit our website at **www.redchairpress.com**.
Find a free catalog of all our high-quality products for young readers.

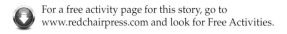

For a free activity page for this story, go to
www.redchairpress.com and look for Free Activities.

Raven Brings Back the Sun

Publisher's Cataloging-In-Publication Data
(Prepared by The Donohue Group, Inc.)

Barchers, Suzanne I.
    Raven brings back the sun : a tale from Canada / retold by Suzanne I. Barchers ;
illustrated by Angela Oliynyk.

    pages : illustrations ; cm. -- (Tales of honor)

    Summary: In the far north of Canada, daylight disappears for much of the year.
This Inuit legend describes how the First Peoples of Canada explained the sun's return
to their remote lands.
    Interest age level: 006-009.
    Issued also as an ebook.
    ISBN: 978-1-939656-80-3 (library binding)
    ISBN: 978-1-939656-81-0 (paperback)

    1. Sun--Juvenile fiction. 2. Ravens--Juvenile fiction. 3. Night—Juvenile fiction. 4.
Folklore--Canada. 5. Sun--Fiction. 6. Ravens--Fiction. 7. Night--Fiction. 8. Folklore--
Canada. I. Oliynyk, Angela. II. Title. III. Series: Barchers, Suzanne. Tales of honor.

PZ8.1.B37 Ra 2015
398.2/73/0971   2014944304

This series first published by:
Red Chair Press LLC   PO Box 333   South Egremont, MA 01258-0333

Printed in the United States of America

WZ1114   1 2 3 4 5 18 17 16 15 14

In the land of the midnight sun, the days of summer can be long and warm. But in the winter, the cold nights linger. To the dismay of the people who lived when the Earth was young, the time of day and light suddenly ended. The sun's light disappeared, and the days remained dark. The only light, whether day or night, came from the distant stars.

In a village near the big water, the people begged the shamans to bring back the sun and the moon. The **shamans** fashioned many charms and **intoned** many chants. But the darkness persisted.

A young orphan boy who lived in the village often sat near the assembly house. He had few friends, for many people thought he was foolish. Some people even treated him poorly. Each day, the boy watched the shamans recreate the same charms and repeat the same chants. Each day, the sun and moon stayed hidden.

One day the boy spoke to the shamans. "Your charms and chants are not working."

The shamans ignored the boy. After all, he was hardly worthy of their notice. Besides, they were occupied with their charms and chants.

The boy spoke again. "Your charms and chants are not working."

"Don't bother us," said a shaman. "Don't you see that we are busy? Our people are counting on us to bring back the light."

"It will take more than charms and chants to bring back the sun and the moon," the boy observed.

"Well, if you think you know so much, why don't you bring back the light?" a shaman grumbled.

"Alright, I will!" declared the boy.

The shamans became angry at the orphan boy's boast and drove him away.

Now, the boy had one possession, a fine black coat that he had made with his own hands. No one knew that once he put on the coat, he had the power to **transform** into a raven. The boy took his coat and went to visit his aunt.

He told her what had happened with the shamans. Then he said, "Tell me where the sun and the moon have gone. I want to bring them back to the people."

"They are hidden somewhere, but I don't know where," replied his aunt.

She noticed his coat he brought with him. "But you hardly need my help. If you could learn to sew that black coat with such fine stitches, you should be wise enough to find the light."

The boy continued to beg her for help. He knew that she was wiser than the shamans.

Finally, his aunt said, "If you truly wish to find the light, you must go far to the south lands. Don't stop walking until you get to where you need to be."

"But how will I know when I'm there?" the boy asked.

"You'll know. Now, take your coat and these snowshoes. You'll need them both. And remember... don't stop until you get there," she said.

The boy left his aunt's home, putting on the coat
and snowshoes as it got colder. He traveled for
many days, while the darkness remained and the
snow fell.

At last, far off in the distance, he saw a soft
ray of light. Encouraged, he kept walking
southward, staying warm in his coat.

As he walked, the light shone brighter. Then it disappeared for a time. Then the light would return. It kept reappearing for short periods, drawing the boy onward.

Finally, the boy came to a large hill. One side of the hill was as dark as the night. The other side was as bright as the day. The boy stopped and stared. He saw a hut with a man shoveling snow in front of it. But he could not see where the light was coming from.

The boy watched for a time before he started down the hill toward the hut.

As the boy approached the hut, he noticed a great ball of fire. He had found the light!

He realized that each time the man tossed snow in the air, the light was **concealed**. As the snow fell away, the light blazed again.

The man saw the boy approaching and stopped his shoveling.

"Good day," said the man. "You look cold and tired. Rest yourself."

"Thank you," said the boy. "But I have a question for you. Why are you throwing up snow and hiding the light?"

The man said, "I'm not hiding the light. I'm just clearing the snow away from my door. But who are you? Where do you come from?"

"I'm from a faraway village to the north. It's so dark there that I left. Can I live here with you?" the boy asked.

"Why do you wish to stay with me?" the man asked in surprise.

"It is too cold and dark up north," replied the boy.

"Then take the shovel and get to work," said the man.

The man turned to enter the hut. He lifted the curtain in front of the door and entered, assuming that the boy was busy shoveling snow.

However, as quickly as the man looked away, the boy caught up the ball of light. He put it under his coat, grabbed the shovel, turned back to the north, and began to run.

21

The man ran out of his hut, shouting, "Stop! Come back here!"

But the boy kept running, running, running. He ran until his legs became tired, hoping that the man would **abandon** the chase.

Realizing that the man was in close pursuit, the boy closed his magic coat and turned into a black raven with large, powerful wings. He flew high in the sky, moving as fast as those wings would carry him.

When the man saw that he could not overtake the raven, he cried out to him. "Alright! Keep the light! But give me back my shovel!"

"No!" the raven boy called out. "You made our village dark. You cannot have the shovel!" And he flew even faster, leaving the man below. Once he was far away, he dropped the shovel.

As the raven boy flew farther away, he tore
a chunk out of the ball of light. He threw the
chunk to the sky, making daylight.

He flew until he was in darkness again.
Then he threw out another chunk of light,
making another day. The raven boy continued
in this way, changing the dark to light as he
flew. Finally he reached his village where he
descended. He then threw the rest of the ball of
light into the sky.

The raven boy took off his black coat, becoming the orphan boy again. As the shamans gathered, they looked at him in wonder.

"As I promised, I have brought back the light. Hereafter, it will be light, then dark, and then light again, so our people will always appreciate the daylight," he pronounced.

And so it is to this day.

abandon:	give up
concealed:	hidden
intone:	to recite in singing tones
shaman:	a person thought to have influence on nature
transform:	to change in form or appearance

WHAT DO YOU THINK?

Question 1: Folktales and myths were often told to explain events of nature. What natural event do you think this tale was told to explain?

Question 2: Why do you think the light appeared as the boy walked further south?

Question 3: How did the boy trick the man?

About Aboriginal Canada

In one of the most remote places in the world, the Canadian Arctic, a people have survived over 1,000 years. They are the Inuit. For the Inuit, the Arctic is a place teeming with life. The name Inuit means "the people." The Inuit are the only Aboriginal people who can be found from one side of Canada to the other.

About the Author

After fifteen years as a teacher, Suzanne Barchers began a career in writing and publishing. She has written over 100 children's books. She previously held editorial roles at Weekly Reader and LeapFrog and is on the PBS Kids Media Advisory Board. Suzanne also plays the flute professionally – and for fun – from her home in Stanford, CA.

About the Illustrator

Angela Oliynyk was born in Ukraine in a family of artists and enjoyed drawing since she was very young. She has worked as a graphic designer and now also as an illustrator. Her inspiration can be traced to her childhood where she lived on a rustic farm with her grandmother, a Ukrainian storyteller. Angela now lives in Montreal, Quebec, Canada and when not making art, she enjoys reading tales, dancing, hiking and skating with her son.